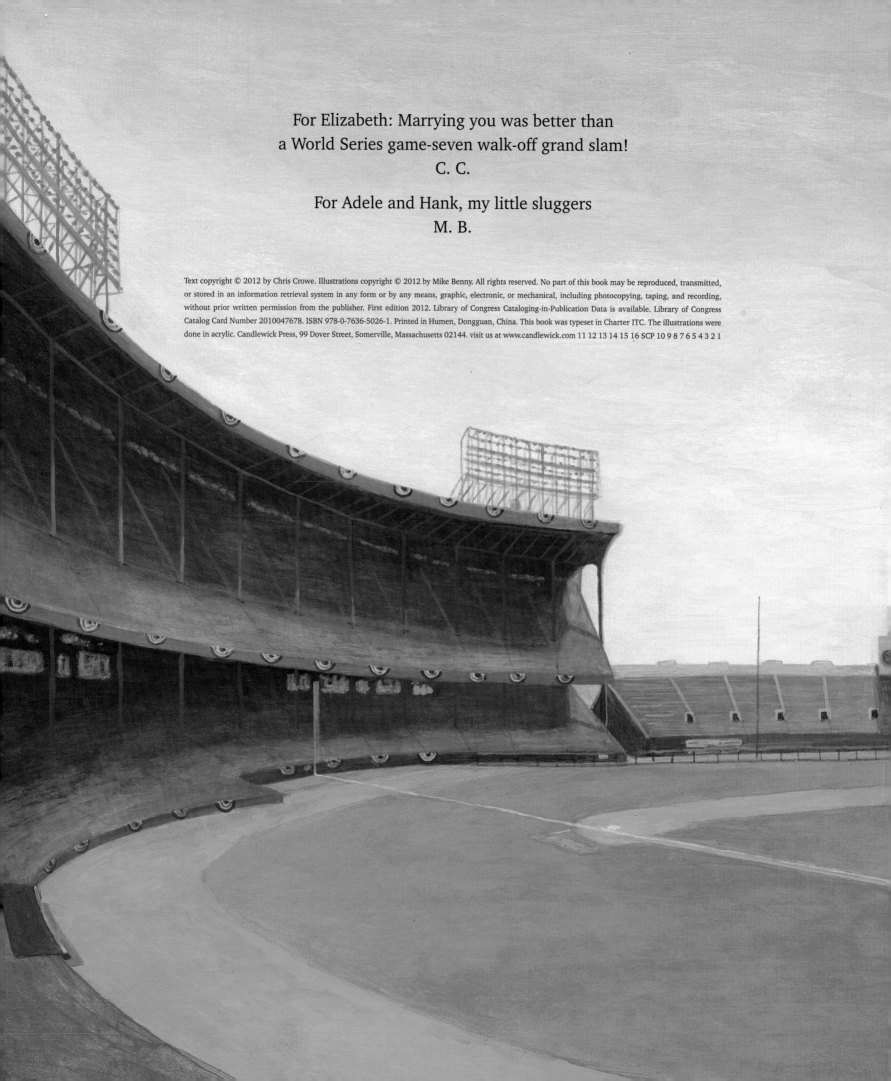

For Elizabeth: Marrying you was better than
a World Series game-seven walk-off grand slam!
C. C.

For Adele and Hank, my little sluggers
M. B.

# JUST as GOOD

## HOW LARRY DOBY CHANGED AMERICA'S GAME

Chris Crowe

illustrated by Mike Benny

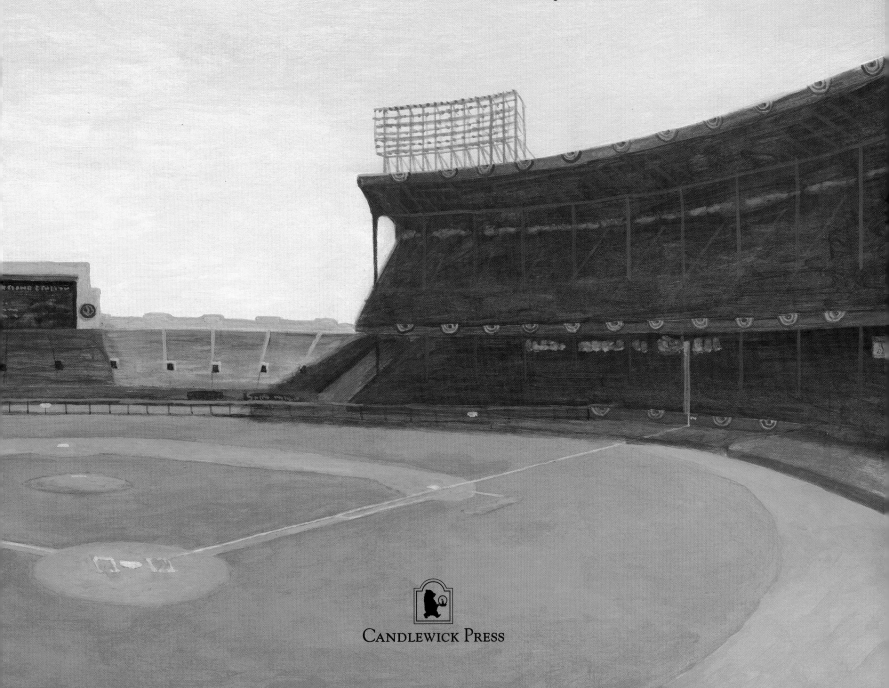

CANDLEWICK PRESS

*DADDY AND I LOVE THE CLEVELAND INDIANS,* and when Larry Doby joined them last season, we both hoped that 1947 would be a year to remember.

"A Negro on our team!" Daddy shouted when he read the news. "First one in the American League."

"It's a miracle!" I said.

***I'd been aching for a miracle*** ever since Coach O'Brien banned me from his Little League baseball team.

"Look around, Homer," he said. "You see any Negroes playing in the major leagues?"

"Jackie Robinson. He's already a star for Brooklyn."

"That boy's a fluke." Coach laughed. "Ain't no other Negro ballplayer worth a spit!"

Right then, I wanted one of our own here in Cleveland playing for my Indians. That'd prove that Jackie's for real, and it'd show that our people are just as good in baseball—or anything else—as whites are.

'Course, I knew it was a crazy dream . . . until Larry Doby showed up.

## Saturday, October 9, 1948

I get up early for my paper route, and Cleveland buzzes with excitement over the World Series; some people are already on street corners scalping tickets for the big game. Others see my Cleveland Indians cap and call out, "How 'bout those Indians!"

I'm hoping to get home soon and finish my chores so I can go down to Standard Drug and listen to the game. If I don't get there early enough, I'll have to stand outside—and that'd be no good at all.

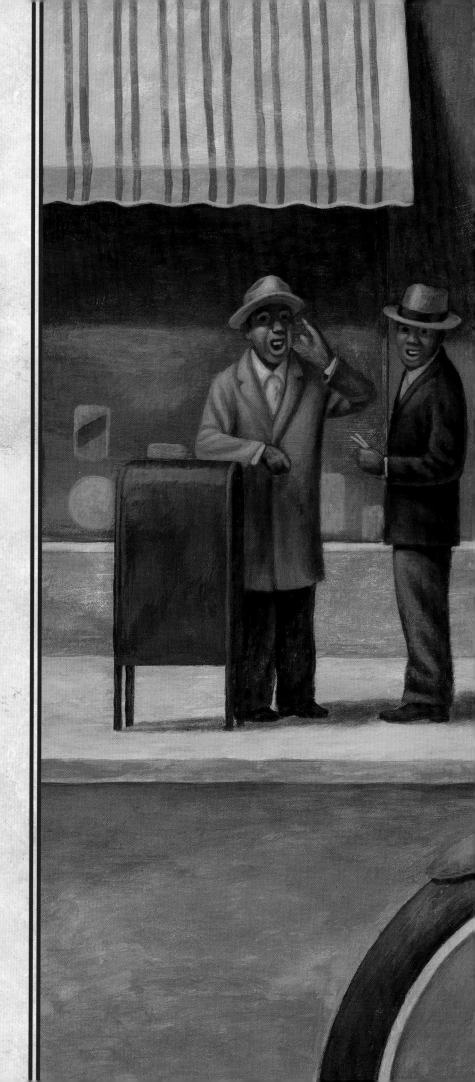

I get home just after one o'clock, and Mama's in the kitchen, shaking her head.

"New radios don't come free," she's telling Daddy, "and we got bills to be paying."

Daddy just smiles and keeps working on that brand-new radio.

I can't believe it! "We got a radio?"

"Won't be as good as being in Cleveland Stadium," Daddy says, "but it sure beats standing in a drugstore."

"You two." Mama chuckles as she leaves the kitchen. "You are baseball crazy."

Daddy's grinning like a birthday boy. "You ready for this, Homer?"

I nod and pull my cap low.

Daddy turns that radio on. The dial glows, and in a few seconds, music floats out.

Daddy starts turning that dial like a safecracker:

News.

Crackly static.

Big-band music.

Then I hear, *"Good afternoon, baseball fans everywhere,"* and my heart thumps.

"That's him, Daddy! Mel Allen! Mel Allen's been calling all the World Series games."

Daddy turns up the radio, and we sit down to listen to the starting lineup. We cheer when we hear that Larry's starting in center field, but Daddy's worried about the pitcher.

"Steve Gromek?" he says. "He'll need help beating the Braves."

"Good thing he's got our man, Larry Doby," I say.

"Our man is THE man." Daddy gives me a thumbs-up.

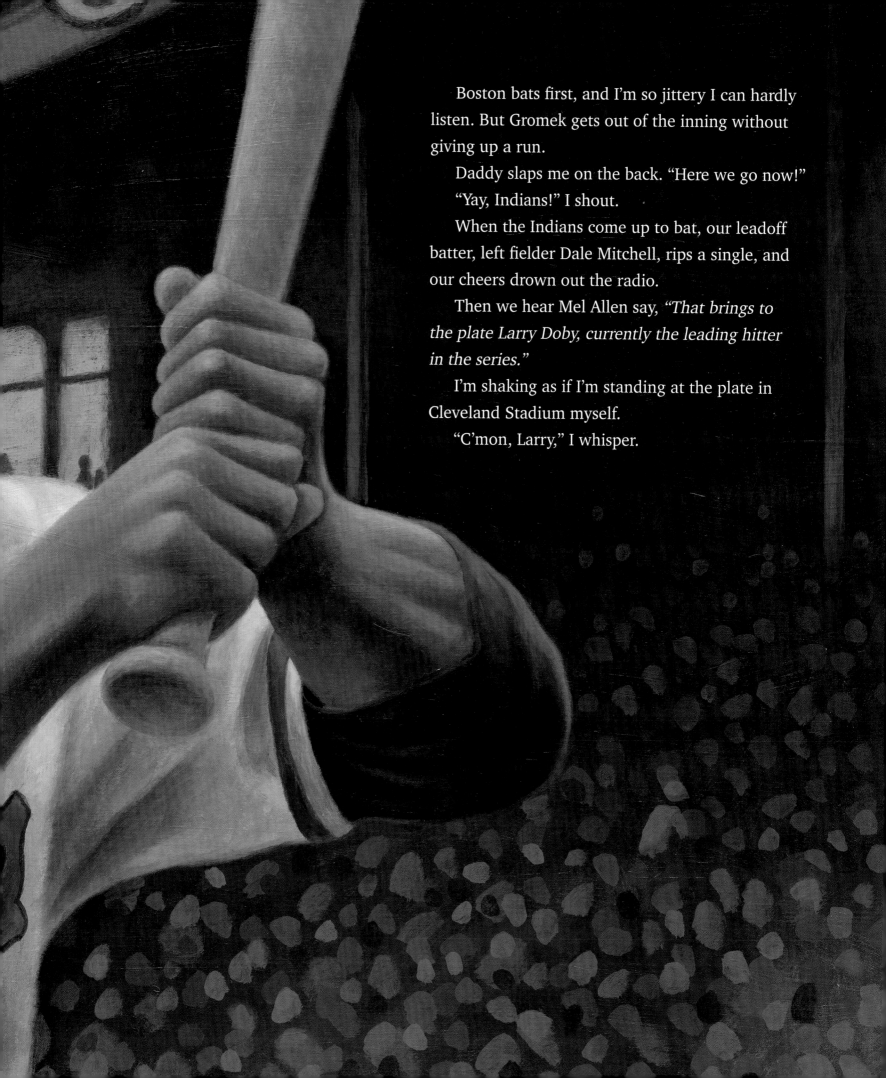

Boston bats first, and I'm so jittery I can hardly listen. But Gromek gets out of the inning without giving up a run.

Daddy slaps me on the back. "Here we go now!"

"Yay, Indians!" I shout.

When the Indians come up to bat, our leadoff batter, left fielder Dale Mitchell, rips a single, and our cheers drown out the radio.

Then we hear Mel Allen say, *"That brings to the plate Larry Doby, currently the leading hitter in the series."*

I'm shaking as if I'm standing at the plate in Cleveland Stadium myself.

"C'mon, Larry," I whisper.

Larry smashes a line drive, and Mel Allen has to shout over the noise of the crowd.

*"Doby's vicious grounder is knocked down . . . and he's out at first!"*

I slump into my chair, but I'm up again when Lou Boudreau, Cleveland's shortstop, drives in a run.

"Way to go!" I shout.

"That's our Indians!" Daddy yells.

Mama sticks her head in the door. "Good news?"

"Mama," I say, "we're already ahead one–nothing!"

She sits down and puts an arm across my shoulders. "Then I'm staying put. Don't want to be missing history."

Nobody scores in the next inning, and Daddy and I start pacing the kitchen.

"We need another run," he says. "Just one more, 'cause there's no way Gromek can keep the Braves from scoring."

In the third inning, Larry Doby comes to bat, and Daddy reaches over and squeezes my hand.

"He's gonna do it," he says. "I can just feel it."

"He'll do it," I tell Daddy. "He's just gotta do it."

Larry swings and misses the first pitch.

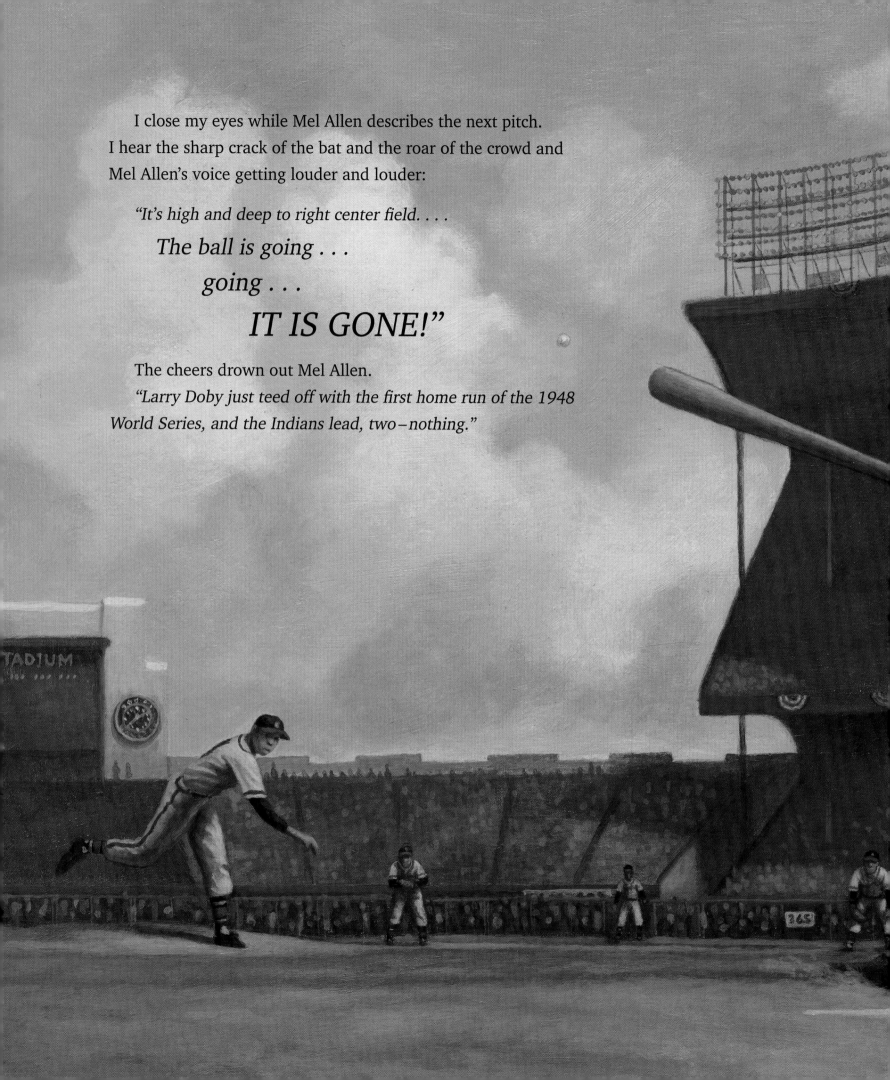

I close my eyes while Mel Allen describes the next pitch.
I hear the sharp crack of the bat and the roar of the crowd and
Mel Allen's voice getting louder and louder:

*"It's high and deep to right center field. . . .*

*The ball is going . . .*

*going . . .*

*IT IS GONE!"*

The cheers drown out Mel Allen.
*"Larry Doby just teed off with the first home run of the 1948*
*World Series, and the Indians lead, two–nothing."*

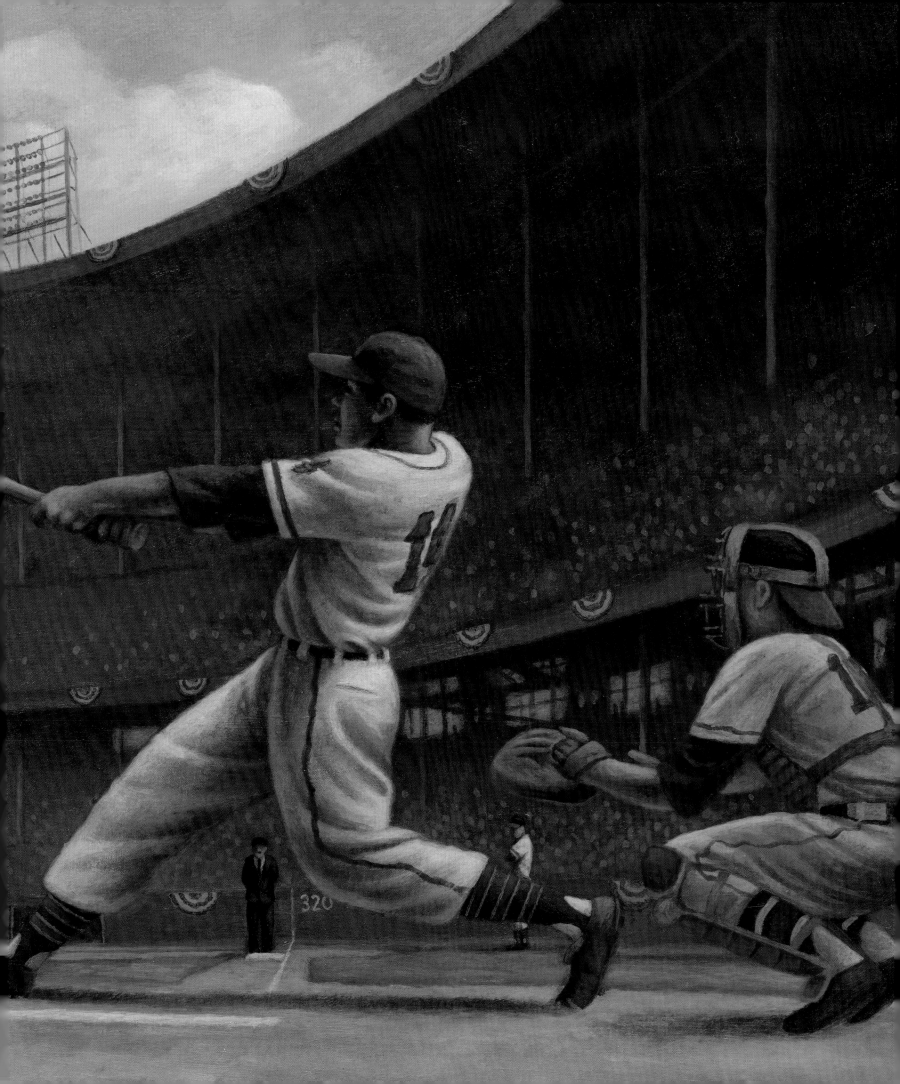

Daddy and Mama and I are dancing in the kitchen, whooping and hollering until our voices go hoarse. Then Daddy pulls Mama into his arms.

"Our man is a World Series hero!" he says.

Mama sits back down to listen while Daddy and I start pacing the kitchen again.

In the seventh inning, Boston's left fielder, Marv Rickert, hammers a home run to make the score two to one, and for the rest of the game, Daddy and I are up and down with every out, pleading with the Indians to hang on to their one-run lead.

Gromek finally gets the last out of the game, and Daddy hugs Mama, then picks me up and twirls me around the kitchen.

"We are on our way!" he says. "Change is a-comin', Homer!"

When he sets me down, I see tears in his eyes.

The next morning, Daddy comes outside to help me fold my newspapers, but what he really wants to do is read about our new hero. He pulls a paper off the stack and turns right to the sports section.

Smack in the middle of the page is a photograph of
Larry Doby and Steve Gromek, celebrating yesterday's win.
Both have smiles as wide as Lake Erie, and they're cheek-to-
cheek, a white face next to a black one, hugging each other
like brothers.

"Look at that," Daddy says. "Will you just look at that?
Change ain't a-comin', Homer. It's already here."

# Historical Note

WHEN LARRY DOBY WAS BORN in South Carolina in 1923, racist Jim Crow laws existed in many states. In much of the nation, it was illegal for African Americans to use "white-only" bathrooms, to attend "white-only" schools, or to eat in "white-only" restaurants: "It shall be unlawful to conduct a restaurant or other place for the serving of food in the city, at which white and colored people are served in the same room."

In some places, Jim Crow laws even applied to baseball: "It shall be unlawful for any amateur white baseball team to play baseball on any vacant lot or baseball diamond within two blocks of a playground devoted to the Negro race, and it shall be unlawful for any amateur colored baseball team to play baseball in any vacant lot or baseball diamond within two blocks of any playground devoted to the white race."

Professional baseball was also affected by Jim Crow; owners of Major League Baseball teams conspired to keep the league all white by refusing to add African Americans to their team rosters.

On April 15, 1947, Jackie Robinson, a star from the Negro Leagues, broke baseball's color barrier when he joined the Brooklyn Dodgers of the National League and became the first African American to play in the modern major leagues. Just eleven weeks later, Larry Doby signed with the Cleveland Indians and became the first black player in the American League.

All season long, both men received abuse from racist players, coaches, and fans.

*"The things I was called did hurt me. They hurt a lot.*
*The things people did to me, spitting tobacco juice on*
*me, sliding into me, throwing baseballs at my head.*
*The words they called me, they do hurt." —Larry Doby*

Many baseball team owners and fans considered Jackie Robinson a fluke. In order to keep teams all white, they claimed that Robinson, the 1947 Rookie of the Year, was a rare exception, that no other African-American players were good enough for the major leagues.

Doby's disappointing rookie season reinforced those racist claims.

But 1948 would be different. Doby's sixteen home runs and .301 batting average helped the Cleveland Indians win their first World Series since 1920. More important, by proving that Robinson was no fluke, Larry Doby, number 14, paved the way for dozens of other African Americans to join him and Jackie Robinson in the major leagues.

In the locker room celebration after game four of the 1948 World Series, Steve Gromek, Cleveland's winning pitcher, hugged Doby right in front of newspaper photographers. The cameras caught their two joyful faces—one white, one black, cheek-to-cheek—and the photograph appeared in newspapers all over America. The picture of a white man hugging a black man angered many people, but for others it signaled that change was coming; if white baseball players could accept African Americans as equals, perhaps the rest of the country could too.

> *"That [hug by Gromek] made me feel good because it was not a thing of 'should I or should I not?', not a thing of black or white. It was a thing where human beings were showing emotion."* —Larry Doby

That photograph and Larry Doby's success helped to tumble the barriers that had pre-vented African Americans from playing in the major leagues. The integration of professional baseball by Jackie Robinson, Larry Doby, and the African-American players who followed them laid the foundation for the civil rights movement, which eventually eliminated Jim Crow laws from American society.

> *"Integration in baseball started public integration on trains, in Pullmans, in dining cars, in restaurants in the South, long before the issue of public accommo-dation became news."* —Branch Rickey, president, Brooklyn Dodgers, 1943–1950

One of the first African-American players to benefit from Doby's success was Satchel Paige, the Negro League's most famous pitcher. Paige became Doby's teammate on July 9, 1948, and finished the regular season with a six-one record. He faced two batters in the seventh inning of game five of the 1948 World Series, becoming the first African-American pitcher to play in a World Series game. The Indians lost that game eleven to five but went on to beat the Boston Braves in game six to win the 1948 World Series four games to two.

# Bibliography

BOOKS AND ARTICLES

Berkow, Ira. "As Good as He Was, Doby Might Have Been Better." *New York Times,* March 8, 1998.

*Cleveland Plain Dealer,* "Details as Indians Near World Title," October 10, 1948.

Drebinger, John. "Gromek Trips Sain." *New York Times,* October 10, 1948.

*Ebony,* "The Future of Negroes in Big League Baseball," May 1949.

Heaton, Charles. "Gromek Bears Down in 9th to Reach Goal." *Cleveland Plain Dealer,* October 10, 1948.

Lewis, Franklin. *The Cleveland Indians.* New York: Putnam, 1949.

Lopez, John P. "Batting Second: Doby Relates to Sacrifices after Following Robinson's Footsteps." *Houston Chronicle,* April 13, 1997.

Maraniss, David. "Neither a Myth Nor a Legend; Larry Doby Crossed Baseball's Color Barrier—After Robinson." *Washington Post,* July 8, 1997.

Moore, Joseph Thomas. *Pride against Prejudice: The Biography of Larry Doby.* New York: Greenwood, 1988.

*New York Times,* "Larry Doby, Ace Negro Infielder, Signs Contract With Cleveland." July 4, 1947.

Tygiel, Jules. "Those Who Came After." *Sports Illustrated,* June 26, 1983.

Veeck, Bill, and Ed Linn. *Veeck—as in Wreck.* New York: Putnam, 1962.

Young, A. S. "Doc." *Great Negro Baseball Stars and How They Made the Major Leagues.* New York: A. S. Barnes, 1953.

———. "Larry Doby Outstanding Star As Indians Win World Series." *Cleveland Call and Post,* October 16, 1948.

AUDIOVISUAL MATERIALS

*10/09/1948 Boston Braves @ Cleveland Indians, World Series Game 4.* MLB.com Baseball's Best, MLBCRBCD25, MLB Advanced Media, LP, 2002. Audio disks.

*Indians: 1948 Cleveland Indians vs. Boston Braves.* Vintage World Series Films, Major League Baseball Properties, 2007. DVD.

ON THE WEB

"1948 World Series: Cleveland Indians vs. Boston Braves." Major League Baseball. http://mlb.mlb.com/mlb/baseballs_best/mlb_bb_gamepage.jsp?story_page-bb_48ws_clebob.

"1948 World Series." Baseball Almanac. http://www.baseball-almanac.com/ws/yr1948ws.shtml.

"Jim Crow Laws." National Park Service. Martin Luther King Jr. National Historic Site. http://www.nps.gov/malu/forteachers/jim_crow_laws.htm.

| DATE DUE | | |
|---|---|---|
| | | |
| | | |
| | | |
| | | |
| | | |
| | | |
| | | |
| | | |
| | | |
| | | |
| | | |
| | | |
| | | |
| | | |
| | | |
| | | |